BOOK OF THE FILM

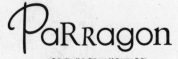

Bath · New York · Cologne · Melbourne · Delhi
Hong Kong · Shenzhen · Singapore

This edition published by Parragon Books Ltd in 2017

Parragon Books Ltd
Chartist House
15–17 Trim Street
Bath BA1 1HA, UK
www.parragon.com

ISBN 978-1-4748-7173-0

Printed in the UK

BOOK OF THE FILM

GUARDIANS OF THE GALAXY Vol. 2

Written and Directed by James Gunn

Based on the Marvel Comics by Dan Abnett and Andy Lanning

Produced by Kevin Feige

PROLOGUE

The hazy summer sun glinted off the hood of the orange-and-teal convertible as it made its way along the winding road, following the Missouri River. It was nearing dusk, and a love song blared from the car stereo as it sped past maple trees, leaving the branches swaying in the wind.

In the passenger seat of the car, Meredith Quill laughed and sang along, as loud and out-of-tune as her 18-year-old voice would allow.

"Do do do do do do do…." She echoed the beat of the chorus and began to joyfully dance in her seat.

Next to her, the well-dressed driver, who looked older than her, yet ageless somehow, laughed. He reached over and brushed a stray strand of her fine blonde hair from her mouth.

She held his hand briefly then leaned in to sing into his hand like a microphone. She sang louder until both were overcome with fits of laughter.

Still smiling, the driver turned off the road and parked beside an ice cream store that stood alone, tucked away in a quiet area far from town.

"Ice cream for dinner? Sounds like a perfect idea to me." Meredith smiled as she hopped out of the car. But the man wasn't headed towards the shop. He walked past the lonely structure towards the edge of the woods behind it. There, he stood patiently, waiting for his companion, his hand outstretched.

An adventure, Meredith thought. Even better than ice cream for dinner. She would go on any adventure with this man.

Gently taking her hand, the man guided Meredith down a steep hillside, snaking their way between the trees. "This way, my river lily."

The two walked further into the forest. "Where are you taking me?" Meredith asked, barely able to hide the excitement in her voice. The man simply nodded ahead as they continued to walk, finally stopping in front of a particular tree. He waved his arm toward it with a flourish.

Meredith looked at it, puzzled. There was nothing spectacular or even out of the ordinary about this tree. It appeared to be just like all of the others in the forest surrounding them – tall, sturdy, beautiful, but still, just a tree.

"I don't understand – what does this –" she began to ask.

The man gently took her chin in his palm and directed her gaze downward, toward the base of the tree, and suddenly, Meredith understood. Or at least, she thought she understood. He hadn't brought her here to look at a tree. What exactly it was she was looking at, she didn't know, only that it took her breath away.

Nestled in the mossy grass of the forest was an unusual sprout, one that definitely did not belong in these woods. In fact, it didn't seem to belong in any forest or jungle anywhere on this Earth. Merely a few centimetres tall, the pattern of its limbs was impossibly complex and uniquely delicate.

"Oh, my. It's so beautiful," she whispered, afraid her voice would cause it to collapse.

She glanced up to see the man standing above her. He had been staring at the magnificent sprout, but now he looked directly into her eyes. She let herself get lost in his gaze. His eyes were so deep, so unfathomable. It was clear from the way they glinted and sparkled that, much like this sprout, he was not of this planet. If she stared at him long enough, she could almost feel herself being lifted off the earth and flying through space.

"Do you like it?" he asked, shaking her

from her trance.

"I do," she said softly.

"I was afraid its roots wouldn't take to the soil, but it has. Far more quickly than I thought." He looked up, pensive, beyond the canopy of the trees to the sky above. "Soon, it will be everywhere. All across the universe, fulfilling life's one true purpose."

Meredith was taken in by his words. "Which is what?" she asked.

"Expansion."

The single word hung in the air, larger than the two of them. Before she could process it, the man swept Meredith into his arms and gazed deeply into her beautiful brown eyes. She felt so overcome with emotion that she had to blink the tears away.

"I – I'm not sure what you're talking about," she said, her voice catching, "but I like the way you say it."

The man held her tighter. "No matter what is to come, know this. My heart is yours, Meredith Quill."

Looking up at him, Meredith said in a far-off voice, "I can't believe I fell in love with a spaceman."

And with that, he bent down and kissed her, as no other man had. As their kiss grew deeper, the plant at their feet slowly began to change. It twitched and twisted, beginning to grow. Meredith's eyes were closed, but if she had been looking at the plant as it danced and unfurled, she would have seen it was no ordinary plant at all. More than just leaves and branches, at its core glowed a light that seemed to radiate from its very essence.

The light continued to spread out from the plant, dancing, beginning to fulfil their destiny....

Chapter 01

An interdimensional crack ripped open a section of space momentarily before quickly closing again with a thunderous clap.

Parked not far from the tear in the universe was the spaceship Milano, its sleek, orange-and-teal design reminiscent of a certain convertible that raced through the winding roads of a planet on the other side of the galaxy over 30 years ago. Beyond the colours, though, the two vehicles and their passengers couldn't be more different. Mostly.

"That was close. You sure about this, Quill?" asked Rocket as he finished buckling up his space rig and jetted closer to the Milano's PA system, secretly ripping out wires, a sly grin on his furry face.

"It'll be here any minute," answered Peter Quill, the ship's captain. Peter was monitoring a red dot on a homemade device crafted from an old handheld videogame he had carried with him since childhood.

"Which will be its loss." Gamora, one of the most fearsome assassins in the galaxy, was wearing a space rig, like Rocket and Quill, as she checked and double-checked a very deadly-looking long-range gun.

"Is that a rifle?" Quill asked, a little surprised.

"You don't know what a rifle is?" Gamora was equally surprised.

"Of course I – I just thought your thing was a sword," he retorted.

Gamora looked at Quill as if this was his first battle. "We've been hired to stop an interdimensional beast from feeding on those batteries' energy and I'm going to stop it with a sword?"

She brushed past him and continued working on her weapon.

"Hey, don't get all huffy," Quill mumbled. "You're the one being inconsistent here."

But she was right – they had to focus on the battle. He looked around, surveying their mission: guarding the batteries that powered the large conductor towers surrounding them. These power stations were massive, and the batteries were some of the most sought-after sources of energy in the galaxy. Which was why the Guardians of the Galaxy had been hired for this job. The batteries were a source of both pride and power for their clients, helping to maintain the beauty and balance of their home world: the Sovereign.

The Sovereign was a magnificent planet,

so perfect it was obviously not made by nature. Light glinted off its golden surface, which was made of interlocking orbs rotating in flawless harmony as it orbited a blue sun. The things Peter Quill saw in his travels across the galaxy never ceased to amaze him.

His wonder was quickly shaken by a much louder, much closer crack that rang out between the dimensions.

"I am Groot," said a young sapling near Quill's boots. Groot, just under 30 centimetres tall, had been freed from his pot, but was still far from being his old self.

"I agree, pal," Rocket replied. "Sounds like it's right on our tail!"

Gamora looked at Drax. The muscled warrior stood with his blades drawn, looking up at the sky. She pointed to his chest. "Drax, why are you standing there? Suit up with one of Rocket's aero-rigs."

Drax shook his head. "It hurts."

"Hurts?" Gamora had no issues with hers and she was a quarter of his size.

"I have sensitive nipples," he muttered, much to the delight of Rocket, who burst into loud laughter.

"Aw, poor baby," Rocket teased. "You wanna bottle?"

Drax snorted. "What about you? What are you doing over there?"

Rocket held up Quill's tape player, loaded with his Awesome Mix Vol. 2 cassette. "If I rig this just right, we can listen to tunes while we blow up whatever wants to come through those cracks," he said, going back to work on the ship's PA system. "Then we can do our job, and get out of here." Rocket turned to Drax. "You're welcome."

"Welcome?" Drax repeated. "How is this a priority?"

"Ask Quill," Rocket said. "He's the one

who likes music so much."

Quill got in between the two, trying to defuse the situation. "I gotta go with Drax on this one, Rocket. You could be checking weapons or something other than this."

"Oh, sure, okayyyy, Quill," Rocket said, winking at him. Then he went back to work on the PA system.

Quill shook his head. "No, Rocket, I seriously agree with Drax."

"Sure," Rocket said, looking back. "I know." He winked again.

"I can clearly see you winking," Drax growled fiercely.

Rocket furrowed his brow. "Wait, I thought I was using my left eye?"

Any further discussion of the sound system was quickly ended by a massive crack, the largest yet. It shook them all, as though space itself tilted slightly.

Quill surveyed his team. It was now or never. Time to lead the Guardians of the Galaxy in another epic battle.

"I am Groot." The little tree jumped up on Rocket and gripped his shoulder.

"Don't worry, pal," Rocket said, pausing his work. "Whatever it is, I'm sure it can't be…." Rocket trailed off as Groot turned him around.

"I am Groot," he said, pointing.

Rocket had crossed paths with some rather nasty creatures in his day. Usually, he ended up in a firefight with them, and usually he won. But the pale, pink monstrosity spilling out of the extradimensional crack in space was most definitely not like anything he'd ever battled before. This was not going to be an easy win in a simple firefight. Fortunately, he had friends. With guns, and blades, and jet packs. And some music to accompany them.

With the press of a button, an upbeat rock

song came blaring over the Milano's PA system. Rocket grabbed his gun and smiled. Now for the fun part, he thought.

Quill gave the order. Turning to his fellow Guardians, he said, "Okay, so we've faced bigger. Or not. But we've got this, so let's kick some space-creature butt!" He reached up, turned on the mask that covered his face for extra protection, and led the charge.

Guns blazing, Gamora, Quill and Rocket used their space rigs to manoeuvre out of the creature's way. They fired upon the beast, trying to pierce its hide. Drax, with a mighty cry, leaped at it holding his twin blades.

The creature, an Abilisk as it was known and feared throughout the galaxy, fed off large energy sources. Every time it opened its mouth and roared, powerful piercing waves escaped through its teeth. This Abilisk was fully grown, almost 40 metres from mouth to tail. The only thing standing between it and one of the most powerful energy stations in this corner of space were the Guardians of the Galaxy.

It was not a fair fight.

Dodging and weaving, the Guardians tried finding a weak spot, blasting everywhere, but the beast was just too massive and overpowering. Diving into another attack, Drax was flung back with a powerful blow, crashing near Groot and destroying the PA system. The music stopped.

"I am Groot?" asked the sapling.

"No, little one, it is best you stay out of this, we don't want you getting swallowed up," Drax assured Groot. Suddenly, an idea struck. He bellowed out to his fellow Guardians: "The beast's hide is too thick. Our weapons do nothing from the outside. I must cut through it from the INSIDE!"

Before the other Guardians could register

what Drax was planning to do, the warrior let out a glorious roar, charged directly at the Abilisk's mouth, and was swallowed whole.

"Great. Giant pinkie here just swallowed our teammate. Ideas, Quill?" Rocket asked, firing away.

"What is he thinking?" Quill asked Gamora.

"He thinks he can pierce the beast from the inside of the skin," said Gamora.

"But that doesn't make any sense," Quill replied. "The skin's the same thickness inside and out!"

Gamora gave him a look that said Duh! "I understand that. So what are we going to do?"

Quill was wondering now how they would be able to complete their mission and save their short-term-planning teammate. He scanned the Abilisk, looking for any sign of damage they may have done. Luck, which had gotten him this far in life, paid off when he noticed something on the creature's neck.

"Gamora – there!" he yelled. "On the neck. Not very big but –"

"I see it," Gamora said coolly. "Get its attention. I will take care of the rest."

Quill jetted up into the sky. "Rocket, get it to look up!"

Rocket began firing with both guns and yelling taunts in every language he could think of. The beast roared and colourful waves of energy flew from its mouth. Rocket dodged just in time, his tail singed.

Attacking from the other side, Quill was shooting and trying to expose the Abilisk's neck. "Look up here, you big sea-monkey!" he shouted at the beast.

Suddenly, the creature turned and lunged at Quill.

Gamora aimed, ready to take her shot.

Nothing. Her rifle was jammed! Without a second thought she threw down the weapon and pulled out her sword. Getting a running start, she leaped onto the creature's neck, plunging her sword into the wound and slicing open its muscular throat.

It gave out a final scream as it crashed onto a platform and died.

Still nursing his bruised tail, Rocket went over and kicked the creature's head. "Ha!" he cried. "Take that!"

Jetting over to Gamora, Quill grinned. "Sword? See? Consistency," he said with a smug smile. "Maybe we should'a tried that from the start."

Gamora folded up her blade, not amused. "You're questioning my abilities on the field of battle?" she snapped. "Who was it that –"

The pair were interrupted by the sound of the Abilisk stirring. They both instinctively reached for their weapons. Suddenly, from the open wound, Drax tumbled out. Standing, he raised his arms in victory.

"Ha! See? I have single-handedly vanquished the beast!"

The Guardians gave him one look and turned away while rolling their eyes. Groot picked up a small piece of debris and threw it at him.

"What?" Drax asked, as the Guardians jetted back to the Milano to clean up before meeting with their client. "You're welcome."

Chapter 02

Peter Quill had been to many planets in the twenty-plus years since a mysterious ship had taken him from Earth. Orphaned from his family, he was raised by the blue-skinned Ravager known as Yondu. The Ravagers scoured every bit of the galaxy looking for treasure, lost items, and sometimes stolen items they kept for themselves. Quill had learned the customs of multiple races and the reputations of countless more. This knowledge – and his own personal charm, he liked to think – kept him alive, even long after he left the Ravagers.

It was also what would keep his team alive here on the Sovereign planet. If they followed his lead.

"Look, guys. Trust me on this. Be extra careful of what you say around these guys," Quill warned.

"Why are you looking at me?" Rocket said defensively. "It's not like I'm gonna get us killed or anything."

"Actually, the Sovereign are easily offended, and the punishment is death," Peter corrected him.

Drax snorted. "Sounds judgmental for a bunch of golden morons."

Peter shushed the warrior and looked around quickly to see if anyone had heard him. "See," he said, "that's the kind of thing you might want to keep to yourself."

"I'll hold my tongue," Gamora said with an icy tone. "As long as they deliver what was promised."

"If they hold such standards, they should

be grateful to us, after we defended their ... what were they called again?" Drax asked, as they made their way to the temple.

"Anulax batteries," Quill answered.

"Harbulary batteries," Drax repeated, sort of.

"Okay, that's nothing like what I said. Important thing is they're worth thousands of units a piece." Peter was beginning to think he should have come alone on this part of the mission. "New plan," he said, "let me do all the talking."

The Sovereign citizens were all gold-skinned and impeccably dressed in the finest clothes in the galaxy that fitted their well-toned bodies. They walked with grace, their movements like a dance, their feet seeming to barely touch the ground. The jewels that adorned them complemented each citizen as if they were specifically made for him or her.

The Guardians entered the main chamber of the High Priestess Ayesha, and even Rocket's breath caught in his throat. Of all of the citizens they had seen so far, she was the closest thing to perfection. The chambermaids and servants surrounding her paled in comparison.

She stood to greet them and Quill awkwardly offered a half-bow.

"High Priestess Ayesha. You're looking very, uh, nice today," he stammered.

"Nice?" Her voice was both cool and questioning.

"That is, I mean, umm, better than nice? Very … pretty?" Quill was at a loss for words.

Ayesha looked down on him from her raised perch and a slight smirk flickered across her face.

"Every Sovereign citizen is born exactly as designed by the community, impeccable, both physically and mentally," she said, an air of pride surrounding her.

"Sounds complicated, but you seem to be doing good so far," Quill said, not sure if she was waiting for an answer.

"We control the DNA of our progeny, germinating them in birthing pods," Ayesha continued, still with an air of pride.

"I guess I prefer making people the old-fashioned way," Peter joked, immediately wishing he could take the words back, fearful he had insulted her.

"Well, Peter Quill," High Priestess Ayesha said, "perhaps someday you could give me a history lesson in the archaic ways of our ancestors. For academic purposes."

Quill was confused. Was she flirting with him? "Yeah, I mean, if it's for research, that could be pretty –"

A sideways glance at Gamora staring at him stopped Quill mid-sentence. "Pretty much not my kind of thing. The whole casual –"

Gamora gave an exasperated sigh and muttered, "Oh, please," before stepping in front of Peter and addressing Ayesha. "Your people promised something in trade for our services. Bring it and we shall gladly be on our way."

Ayesha turned her gaze to the green-skinned woman, her head tilting in near-admiration at Gamora's boldness. Looking to her guards, she nodded. A few seconds later two guards returned with a woman, her head covered by a hood, her wrists shackled together. Pushing her to her knees, one of the guards ripped off the hood from her face.

It was the deadly assassin, Nebula!

She took a moment for her eyes to adjust to her surroundings. Looking behind her, she saw the High Priestess's dispassionate gaze. In front of her, she saw a group of well-armed warriors. She had traded one set of captors for another. She recognized the Guardians of the Galaxy, one in particular who was glaring fiercely at her. She curled her lips and stared back at Gamora.

"Family reunion. Yaaaay," Peter muttered.

"I believe she is your sister," Ayesha stated to Gamora, who was approaching Nebula.

Grabbing Nebula roughly and lifting her to her feet, Gamora sneered. "She's worth no more to me than the bounty due for her on Xandar." She barely acknowledged her sister. Nebula did her best to do the same.

Ayesha waved the sisters off, seeming to be glad to see the last of something so beneath her. "Our soldiers apprehended her attempting to steal some Anulax batteries. Do with her as you please."

As the Guardians began to file out of the chamber, Quill made another awkward bow. "Thank you, High Priestess Ayesha," he said, and turned to go as well.

"Mister Quill," Ayesha's voice rang out,

stopping him, "what is your heritage?"

Peter seemed taken aback by the question. "My mother is from Earth," he said.

"And your father?" Ayesha pressed.

Quill paused. "He's ... not from Missouri," he said. "That's all I really know." He shifted his feet from side to side uncomfortably. This was not a topic he liked to dwell on, much less talk about with Sovereign priestesses.

Ayesha stared at him intently, as if she were studying him, able to see his very DNA. Her face turned into a sneer of near-disgust. "I see it within you, your unorthodox genealogy," she said. "A hybrid that seems particularly ... reckless."

Quill felt the sting of her words on his face. "Wait a sec," he started, "just a minute ago you wanted to, you know, make science with me and stuff and now...." His blood began to boil, but he remembered his earlier warning to his team about insulting the Sovereign. "Never mind. See you never, lady."

Quill stomped past Rocket, who followed him out of the chamber, but not before turning to address the High Priestess. "You know, they told me you people were a bunch of goldenrods with sticks up your butts," he said casually. "But that isn't true at all."

The entire team froze. Rocket winked at Drax before he realized: "Oh man, I'm using the wrong eye again aren't I?" Turning back to Ayesha, he offered an apology in his own way. "I'm sorry," he said. "That was meant to be behind your back."

Ayesha stared at them for a long moment and then, with the slightest gesture, dismissed them with a quick wave of her hand. Quill and Gamora quickly hurried out with Nebula, followed closely by Rocket and Drax.

"Count yourself blessed they didn't kill

you," said the big warrior.

"Heh, that's nothing, pal," Rocket replied with a mischievous grin. "We got the last laugh." He rolled up his sleeve slightly to reveal five stolen Anulax batteries!

Drax's eyes widened and he began to laugh, but Rocket hushed him as he returned his contraband into hiding.

Back at the Sovereign space dock, the Guardians boarded the Milano, nestled among the Sovereign's fleet of sleek, capsule-shaped ships. Like everything about the Sovereign, they looked as though they were meant to slice through space with exact precision. Rows and rows of ships lined the dock.

With everyone on board, Rocket guided the Milano away from the golden planet just as the blue sun began to set.

Chapter 03

Usually the music from the Awesome Mix Vol. 2 was enough to brighten Peter Quill's mood. Or at least take his mind off whatever might be bothering him. But as the Milano flew out of the Sovereign's orbit, not even the bouncy, up-tempo song playing from the repaired PA system's speaker could shake his mood.

Quill seemed to be in a wrestling match with his jacket as he tried to shake it off. Finally freed, he threw it on the ground as Gamora passed by. "You all right?" she asked. "Or did the jacket offend you and you've now taken up the Sovereign customs?"

"The Sovereign?" Quill spat the words

in disgust as he flopped into a seat on the flight deck.

"That High Priestess did seem to overstep her bounds," Gamora reflected.

"Right?" Quill sat up, his face momentarily flushed. "That stuff about 'reckless hybrid'. Hey lady, people who live in glass houses shouldn't throw stones." He leaned back in his seat. "And that stuff about my father?" he continued. "Who does she think she is?"

Gamora put her hand on his arm. "I know you're sensitive about that."

"I'm not sensitive about it," Peter said, a little too forcefully to cover the lie. "I just don't know who he is."

Gamora nodded at him. Being the adopted daughter of the mad and fearsome Thanos, she didn't feel it was her place to offer any advice on parentage.

Registering the touch of Gamora's hand on

his arm, Quill suddenly recalled the scene from earlier. "Oh, man, Gamora," he said awkwardly. "Sorry if it looked like I was flirting with her back there. I wasn't. I just started talking and she was talking about baby-making and –"

Gamora removed her hand from Peter's arm. "I don't care if you were flirting," she said, her tone unreadable.

Peter leaned in, a playful glint in his eye. He could never resist the chase. "See, I think you do care," he insisted. "That's why I'm apologizing."

Gamora got up and moved towards the back of the ship, grabbing Nebula by the chains along the way.

"Still sorry!" Quill called after her. He watched her leave and then leaned back, smiling. His mind went back to the time when he introduced Gamora to music on Knowhere. The balcony, the starlight. Even thinking of the battle earlier, when she used her sword to slay the Abilisk with no hesitation, made his smile grow into a goofy grin. The way she used her sword, it seemed so natural. He could still feel her hand on his arm. It felt as if –

"Gamora is not the one for you, Quill."

Quill's thoughts were abruptly interrupted by Drax, standing over him.

"I wasn't … she and I … we're not –" Quill stammered.

"You were staring at her the way a man stares at the woman he wants, were you not?" Drax asked.

"I wasn't staring," Quill said defensively.

"There are two types of beings in the universe," Drax continued, ignoring him, "those who dance, and those who do not."

"Uh huh." Quill wasn't sure where Drax was going with this, which was not unusual whenever Drax began to tell one of his tales.

Drax looked out of the window, gazing at the stars. "I first met my beloved at a war rally. Everyone in the village flailed about, their arms and legs in every direction. Dancing. Except one woman. My Ovette. I knew immediately she was the one."

"Because your thing is being a buzzkill?" Quill asked, genuinely confused.

"The most melodic song in the world could be playing and she wouldn't even tap her foot," Drax answered plainly. "She wouldn't move a muscle. She was so still among so many people dancing about, one might assume she was dead." Drax smiled at the thought.

"Well, yeah, I can see how that's pretty hot –" Quill lied.

"It would make my heart race and I would want to grab her and take her to bed and –" Drax continued, completely wrapped up in the memory.

"Okay," Quill quickly interrupted, waving his arms. "Fascinating. Beautiful. Love story for the ages. I don't need to know the rest. I get your point. I'm a dancer and Gamora is not."

Drax turned back to Quill, placed his hands on his shoulders, and smiled, saying, "You just need to find a woman who is pathetic. Like you."

The big warrior squeezed Quill's shoulders, then let go and left.

"Great talk. Really," Quill called after him. "Next time I need a pick-me-up I know where to go. Thanks!" Shaking his head, he sneaked a glance down the ship, towards Gamora and Nebula.

In the back of the Milano, Gamora did not go easy or show her sister any kindness as she secured her to the wall. For a moment, both sisters refused to look at each other. Nebula's eyes rested on a bowl of fruit.

"I am hungry," she said. "Hand me some of that yaro root." It was more of a demand than a request.

"No. It is not ripe yet," Gamora answered flatly. "Also, I can't stand you."

"You can't stand me?!" Nebula snapped furiously. "You left me there –"

"You flew away. Your choice," Gamora interrupted.

"Left me there," Nebula continued, ignoring her sister, "while you stole that stone for yourself. Yes, I'm in these chains because I tried to steal, yet here you stand, a 'hero' – some sort of 'Garden of the Galaxy!'"

"Some sort of what?" Gamora asked, not sure what her sister had just said. She and Nebula stared at each other, both confused. Suddenly it dawned on Gamora. "Oh, 'Guardians of the Galaxy'."

"Whatever," Nebula said, trying to

hide her ignorance.

"Why would we be the 'Gardens of the Galaxy?'" Gamora asked, bewildered.

Nebula shrugged. "You have a tree and a furry creature," she said. "I don't know. I thought it was stupid, anyway."

"That it would be," Gamora agreed.

"It's still wordy," Nebula said, trying to provoke her sister.

Gamora shrugged it off and said, "I wasn't the one who thought of it."

Suddenly, Nebula lunged at Gamora, her face stopping mere centimetres away from her sister's. Gamora didn't flinch, knowing the bonds that held Nebula were tight enough to restrain Drax. There was a fire in Nebula's eyes.

"Your name doesn't matter," Nebula spat. "I'll be free of these shackles soon enough, and when I am I'll kill you. I swear it."

Gamora stared into her sister's eyes,

emotionless. "No," she calmly replied. "You'll live out your days in a prison on Xandar, wishing you could."

The sisters stood staring at each other in silence for a few moments, until their stand-off was interrupted by the blaring sound of the ship's alarms. The lights above them began to flash. Gamora ran to the stairs and quickly ascended to the flight deck. She was joined by Drax as the two ran towards the cockpit where Rocket and Quill were already seated.

"Why the alarms?" she asked.

Rocket pointed to the monitor. Gamora's heart leaped to her throat as Quill exclaimed, "Because we have an armed Sovereign fleet on our tail!"

Chapter 04

The Sovereign fleet had a reputation throughout the galaxy for its precision, speed and cunning. The golden, capsule-shaped omnicraft were capped on either end by deadly blasters. Like all Sovereign citizens, their pilots were designed at birth to be nothing short of perfect. The sight of nearly two dozen ships closing in would send anyone into a panic. The crew of the Milano was no exception.

"This is so not good," Quill said, wiping sweat off his brow and trying to think his way out of a firefight with the golden fleet.

"Why are they targeting us?" Gamora asked. "We completed our mission!"

She was baffled as the fleet slowly grew closer.

"Probably because Rocket stole some of their batteries," Drax stated casually.

Rocket whipped his furry head around and shot him a betrayed look. "Dude!"

"Oh, right. He didn't steal those. I don't know why they are after us. What a mystery this is," Drax tried to cover, too late.

Quill and Gamora stared at Rocket, both ready to explode. On the monitors the Sovereign fleet was close enough now to see the video monitors of the pilots' faces, jaws set in determination to destroy those who had dared commit such an affront to them.

Rocket pointed at a screen and shouted, "Incoming!"

Quill steered the ship, barely dodging the blast from the Sovereign omnicraft.

"There's no turning back now, eh?" Gamora sighed.

"What were you thinking?" Quill yelled at Rocket, swiftly evading another blast.

Rocket shrugged. "Dude, they were really easy to steal," he explained.

"That's your defence?" Gamora said, amazed at his audacity. "I should shackle you with Nebula below the deck."

Rocket looked at them as if they were the ones who didn't get it. "Come on," he pleaded. "You saw how that high priestess talked down to us! Especially you, Quill. I'm teaching her a lesson!"

Quill smacked his forehead. "Oh! I didn't realize your motivation was altruism and this was all just Rocket's Good Deed of the Day," he said with exaggerated gratitude. "Such a shame the Sovereign didn't realize it either and are now trying to kill us. My bad."

Rocket sat back, arms crossed, and shouted, "Exactly!"

"I was being sarcastic!" Quill exploded.

"Oh no, you tricked me! You're supposed to use your sarcastic voice! Now I look foolish!" Rocket snapped back.

Drax laughed at Rocket as the creature got more and more flustered.

"Shut up, Drax!" Quill shouted. "You knew about this. You're just as guilty that we're in this mess." Quill fumed, swerving to avoid another Sovereign blast.

Gamora slammed her hand against the cockpit. "Can everyone just put the bickering on hold until after we survive the massive space battle?" she scolded through gritted teeth.

Rocket and Quill stared at each other for a moment. Rocket cocked his eyebrow, nodding his head back at Gamora. "Wowza," he said. "Someone woke up on the wrong side of the bed this morning."

Quill darkened, not amused, his eyebrows

cinched together. "Do not try to bro down with me right now, dude," he said, his voice strained. "All I want to do is punch you in the face."

"Real nice," Rocket protested, throwing his hands in the air. "Resorting to violence."

"Shut. Up!" Quill hissed. He looked at the monitors and steered away from another omnicraft blast.

"For such a commanding and fearsome presence, these ships sure seem to miss rather often," Gamora mused.

"Thanks for the flying credit," Quill said, slightly offended.

"My point is that these seem to be warning shots," Gamora explained. "If they wanted us dead by now, I feel they would have put more of an effort into it."

"Well, you're about to get to test that theory," Quill said, pointing ahead as another battalion of Sovereign omnicraft appeared in front of them. "More incoming!"

"Good!" Rocket exclaimed, aiming the Milano's guns at the approaching omnicraft. "I wanna fry some guys!" Rocket began firing the ship's guns at the oncoming Sovereign fleet.

The fleet broke formation, deftly avoiding the barrage of gunfire from the Milano. The omnicraft pitched and rolled, their sleek capsule shapes dancing through space between the blasts. A video monitor in the centre of each capsule displayed a Sovereign pilot, determination and focus bred into their DNA. The superiority of the pilots' skills was apparent as their eyes never left their target, despite the rapid-fire shots Rocket was unleashing.

One laser beam flew from the Milano's cannon and sped through space, aimed directly at a Soveriegn omnicraft. The pilot saw it and hesitated slightly. That was his downfall. As the beam collided with the ship, his face on the monitor let out a scream.

Rocket cheered. "Nailed ya, sucker! One dead, now who's next?"

Gamora looked closer at the ships, pointing to the centre where the video monitors were. "No one's dead," she said. "Those faces. They're not in the ships. These are remotes."

"Then I can blow 'em all outta the sky and get even more warm fuzzies," Rocket said with a grin.

Dodging more Sovereign warning blasts, Quill wondered aloud, "If they're not in there, then where are the pilots?"

Back on the Sovereign planet near the flight deck was a large control bay. Inside were rows upon rows of pods, each containing a Sovereign Pilot staring at a video monitor. They manoeuvred flight controls with targeting locks and missile launching buttons as if they were actually inside the omnicraft, yet they were safely controlling each ship from their own pod.

On one monitor, the Milano's cannon blast could be seen headed straight for it. The pilot froze – suddenly, her screen turned to static. She yelled in frustration at her failure. Her cursing cut off abruptly as she looked up at the observation deck. Her commanding officer was giving her a disapproving look; however, it was the figure approaching him that forced her into a silent bow.

High Priestess Ayesha strode directly to the Admiral of her fleet, a displeased look clearly etched on her usually serene face. "What is the delay, Admiral?" she said impatiently.

The Admiral was hesitant. "High Priestess, if we destroy their craft, we run the risk of destroying the batteries," he explained. "As you know, they are extraordinarily combustible and could, in turn, destroy our entire fleet."

Ayesha waved her hand, cutting off further discussion. Turning to the Admiral, her jaw set, she drew to her full height and addressed him: "We have thousands of batteries and thousands of ships. Our concern is avenging their slight against our people. We hire them and they steal from us? The sheer audacity alone is heresy of the highest order."

"Y-yes, High Priestess," the Admiral stammered in the face of her fury.

"Now give the command," Ayesha ordered as she took a step back, her eyes never leaving his.

The Admiral bowed after a moment and moved to the communication station. Flipping a switch so that all pilots could hear him, he spoke into the comm. "All command modules...."

In space, the Guardians watched the video monitors of the Sovereign omnicraft showing the pilots tilting their heads slightly, awaiting their new orders.

The Admiral hesitated slightly as he composed himself enough to speak the words with authority.

"Fire with intent to kill."

Chapter 05

"Die! Die! Die, you gold-skinned suckers!!" Rocket yelled as he swivelled the ship's gun around, blasting at everything in sight.

"I am Groot," said the young sapling in a calming tone.

"Yeah, yeah, pal, I know, I know. These are remotes, not real pilots, blah blah blah." Rocket grinned over at his friend and winked. "That's what makes this even better."

"I suggest less talking and more firing," Drax interrupted. "Their fleet does not seem to be engaging in banter."

Gamora glanced out of the window. She tried her best not to let panic creep into her voice as she warned, "The entire fleet just opened fire."

"Tell me something I don't know!" yelled Quill, concentrating on dodging the sudden barrage of firepower.

"Guess they're done warning us," Rocket said with a gulp as he returned fire.

"You!" Quill snapped at Rocket, still angry about the stolen batteries. "Not another word until –" His outburst was cut off as the Milano suddenly jolted harshly to the left. Alarms blared and the emergency systems went into overdrive.

"That does not bode well," Drax said, stating the obvious.

"You think?" snapped Gamora.

"We've just lost a good portion of our right wing," Quill informed the team.

"There is no way we can continue to outmanoeuvre them. No offence," said Gamora, surveying the huge number of ships now firing on them.

"For once, none taken," Quill muttered. Even he knew he couldn't out-fly this many ships, and they were definitely out-gunned. "Quick, what's the closest habitable planet?"

Gamora stood at a monitor, her fingers dancing across a keyboard, her eyes scanning the planets as they zoomed across the screen. Drax looked over her shoulder.

"There?" Drax pointed.

"He said inhabitable," Gamora said, shoving his hand out of the way. "Not all of us can survive sub-zero temperatures."

Drax grunted and stepped away, his help clearly not appreciated.

"Got one," Gamora called out. "It's called Berhert."

"Sounds lovely. How many clicks?" Quill pressed, his voice getting tenser.

"Only one," Gamora answered, though her voice sounded unconvincing.

"What's the catch?" Quill asked, noting her doubtful tone.

"The access point is through that quantum asteroid field to our left," Gamora replied, delivering the bad news.

Quill looked out and saw what she was referring to. A quantum asteroid field was unlike a normal collection of rock clusters flying through space. That would be difficult enough to fly through. This was a huge field of glowing asteroids that swirled about in random patterns. It comprised of individual asteroids that would disappear, only to emerge again seconds later a few metres away. There was no rhyme or reason to the way a quantum asteroid field operated, making it nearly impossibly to navigate.

With one deft motion, Quill turned the

Milano to the left and headed straight for the chaotic field.

Drax looked at him, equal parts dubious and impressed. "I am amazed, Quill," he said. "To make it through that, you'd have to be the greatest pilot in the universe."

Without taking his eyes off the quantum field, Peter smirked and said, "Lucky for us –"

"I am!" Rocket exclaimed.

With a swift gesture, Rocket flipped the pilot control switch so he was now in charge of navigating the ship.

"What the – give that back!" Quill shouted. "I thought you were having fun with the 'Die! Die! Die!'" He reached for the pilot control switch.

Rocket swatted his hand away. "Your turn to shoot now," he said. "This looks like way more fun."

The ship dived deeper into the quantum asteroid field. Glowing, swirling stones appeared and disappeared in front of them. Rocket veered to the right just as a cluster appeared where the ship had been moments ago. Gamora stifled a gasp. Groot hid under a chair. Drax watched with a grin on his face at the thought of such a glorious escape from certain death.

Behind them, the Sovereign fleet followed into the field. While they were bred to be perfect pilots, recklessness was not in their genetic make-up. The idea of such behaviour was something most pilots were unable to grasp. Those pilots' omnicraft were almost immediately pulverized as the quantum stones crashed into their ships.

On the Sovereign planet, pod after pod saw their monitors go dark as their ships were destroyed in the asteroid field. The pilots climbed out, some hanging their heads in shame, others clearly shaken, while many pounded their now-useless pods in anger. None, however, dared to look up to the observation deck.

Ayesha watched as one after another of her pilots failed her. It was not a sight she was accustomed to and it angered her. She gripped the railing, leaning in, her eyes narrowing as the Milano slipped away from her fleet.

Back in the asteroid field, a battle raged within the Milano for control of the ship. While Rocket concentrated on avoiding an approaching cluster, Quill reached for the switch and flipped it so he was once again piloting. He dived under the cluster at the last second.

"What are you doing?" Rocket demanded furiously.

"I've been flying this rig since I was ten years old!" Quill retorted, expertly dodging an asteroid that suddenly appeared in front of them.

"Well, I was cybernetically engineered to

pilot a spacecraft! Beat that, Earthboy!" Rocket taunted, flipping the control back to himself, then quickly jerking the ship away from an asteroid that nearly collided with them head-on.

"You were cybernetically engineered to be a pain in the butt!" Quill sniped. He took back control and flew over a particularly large glowing rock.

Gamora slammed her hand between the two of them. "Stop it!" she yelled, "before you get us all killed."

Rocket sat back, glaring at her. Then he turned to Quill and said, "Later on tonight you're gonna lay down in your bed and there's gonna be something squishy in your pillowcase and you're gonna be wondering 'Huh, what's this?' and it's gonna be because I put a turd in there."

Gamora sighed and backed away.

Rocket grinned, seeing his opportunity

to reach the unprotected switch. "Gotcha," he muttered triumphantly.

"You put a turd in my bed and I will shave you," Quill threatened.

"Oh, it won't be my turd," Rocket grinned, piloting the Milano through the field. "It'll be one of Drax's."

At this, Drax laughed loudly. Gamora shot him a look. "We're about to die and this is what we're discussing?" she said.

Drax shrugged. "I have famously large waste," he explained. "They raise havoc with the pipes. That's why I do all of the plumbing."

"Enough!" Gamora shouted, fed up.

The Milano continued to dodge and weave erratically through the quantum asteroid field as Rocket and Quill jockeyed for control.

"Give it!" Quill yelled.

"You're the hotshot pilot," Rocket replied. "Try shooting at some of those ships still following us!"

Behind them, the Sovereign omnicraft continued their pursuit, but they were slowly being thinned by the constantly shifting asteroids.

Back on the observation deck, Ayesha was growing impatient. She turned to the Admiral. "This failure is unacceptable," she admonished.

"Respectfully, High Priestess, we couldn't have prepared for a scenario where they would actually attempt such an insane manoeuvre," the Admiral replied. "I doubt they are even aware of the explosive damage their stolen cargo is capable of. If they were, no one in their right mind would have —"

A withering look from Ayesha silenced the Admiral. "I did not ask for an assessment of the hybrid and his crew's mindset," she hissed. "It is time to stop making excuses and start providing successful alternatives."

"Yes, High Priestess," the Admiral answered, quickly moving away to study a map of the surrounding starfield on one monitor and the progress of his remaining pilots on another.

Ayesha stared at the remaining pilots in their pods who were doing everything they could just to manoeuvre through the quantum asteroids, much less stay hot on the tail of the Milano.

"We're nearing the edge of the field," Gamora announced, relief starting to ease into her voice. "And only a handful of Sovereign ships remain."

"Wonderful. Now let me get us out of the homestretch," Quill said, reaching over for the controls.

"No way! I did most of the flying. Who says you get to take the credit at the end?" Rocket yelled, reaching for the control at the same time.

Both pilots had their hands on the switch

for a moment, and in that moment neither had their eyes on the ship's monitor. Before Gamora could shout a warning, a large asteroid SLAMMED into the rear of the Milano, shaking the entire craft.

"We're hit!" Rocket screamed over the deafening alarms.

"Really? What was your first clue, genius?" Quill yelled back. "Where?"

Gamora surveyed the monitors. "Lower rear section," she said, suddenly growing pale.

"What's down there?" Quill asked, as the ship began to pitch about.

"Nebula," Gamora replied, already racing back to reach her sister, but she was slammed against a wall before she could reach the stairwell.

At the back of the Milano, a large chunk of the ship had been ripped away by the collision with the asteroid. Boxes of gear and other cargo that wasn't fastened down were being sucked into the cold vacuum of space.

Nebula floated sideways, her body pulled towards the gaping hole. Her chains, shackled against the far wall, held her in place, keeping her inside the craft. But as the hole began to tear wider, sucking more and more atmosphere and cargo from the ship, Nebula was slowly exposed to the creeping space. Her cries for help went unheard as her face and body began to cover over with frost.

Chapter 06

The Milano was in chaos! The hole grew bigger and bigger as more things went crashing toward the vast emptiness of space. Cargo, supplies and weapons were rapidly being sucked closer to the gaping hole.

"I am Groot!" shouted the young sapling, swept up in a current of air.

"Hold on, buddy!" Peter Quill switched on his Star-Lord mask and reached out his hand towards Groot, who extended a branch in turn, continuing to extend it gradually until both branch and arm clasped. Star-Lord gave a mighty tug and pulled Groot back to safety.

"I am Groot," he said, relieved.

"Yeah, yeah, you are," Star-Lord replied, "but we're not out of this yet." He spotted a flashing button above him. Looking back down at Groot, he said, "Think I can get a lift?"

Groot smiled. Wrapping his branches around Star-Lord's boots, he helped lift him half a metre in the air.

Now face-to-face with the blinking button, Star-Lord slammed his hand against it. Suddenly, a blue energy shield appeared at the back of the ship, extending to cover the hole. Nebula fell back to the floor with a thud.

Star-Lord turned to the other Guardians and slid his mask off. "See? Backup shields," he said with a swagger. Gamora glared at him. From the back of the ship, Nebula's thawing voice yelled, "Idiots!"

"Can we not for about five minutes. All that space vacuuming—" Rocket gave his head a vigorous shake, only to be interrupted by Drax laughing.

Pointing at Rocket, Drax said, "You look like an electrified Orloni!"

Rocket looked at his reflection in the window. It was true. All of his fur was standing on end after being whipped about by air currents.

Rocket scowled. "Well, that's what you get when Quill is flying," he muttered.

Gamora wasn't paying any attention to him. Looking out of the window, she opened her mouth in alarm. "Look – there's another one!"

"Another what?" Quill asked, running back to the cockpit. "Space-worm? Asteroid? Hole in the ship? I need specifics."

"Sovereign ship. And it's closing in fast," Gamora said grimly.

"A fine warrior indeed. I would like to meet this pod-pilot," Drax said, nodding his head, impressed.

"Meet him? He's trying to KILL us," Rocket explained.

"A small matter. Once that is settled, we shall meet," Drax said, crossing his arms, ending any further conversation.

Suddenly, a blast from the Sovereign ship grazed the Milano, and all the lights flickered before going completely dark. Gamora punched a series of codes into the console before slamming her fist down.

"Our weapons are down!" she exclaimed.

"Now we shall see what this pod-pilot can do," Drax said, disappearing towards the back of the ship.

"Gamora, how far off did our detour take us?" Quill asked.

"We're twenty clicks away from the jump point," she replied.

Another blast rocked the ship, this one taking out the left wing. Both Rocket and Quill looked at each other thinking the same thought: Okay, hot shot, get us out of this one! But neither had any idea what to do next.

Out of the corner of his eye, Quill saw Drax descending into the hull of the ship. "Oh, great. We have our first deserter...." he muttered.

"He's gaining on us," Rocket reported. "What do we do without weapons? Should I just start throwing yaro root and Drax poop at him?"

"I'm thinking!" Quill said, running out of options.

"Oh. Quill's thinking. We're dead, for sure," Rocket quipped.

In the back of the ship, Nebula watched Drax approach.

"I'm fine, thanks. Glad someone finally came to check on me," she said bitterly.

"Nebula, I did not know you were here," Drax replied, forgetting about the prisoner they had on board. "I am glad to see you alive." He brushed past her before she could say another

STAR-LORD

The interstellar adventurer known as Peter Quill never imagined he'd one day be known far and wide as *Star-Lord*. But that's exactly what happened after he and his unlikely team of misfits, the *Guardians of the Galaxy*, banded together to save the galaxy. Now, with a new outlook on his place in the universe, a mixtape of fresh tunes and a mystery from the past yet to be solved, Quill sets out with his friends to do something good, something bad – maybe even a bit of both.

ROCKET

A unique genetic creation, the tough-talking Rocket may resemble a certain Earth rodent, but you'd be hard-pressed to find his kind anywhere else in the galaxy. Rocket's feisty attitude still sometimes causes friction with his teammates, though his unique intelligence in mechanics and engineering usually makes up for any of his annoying habits.

GROOT

After his heroic sacrifice during the Guardians' first adventure, the tree-like being known only as Groot is now in the process of re-growing his body from a single twig. Though once a towering giant, Groot's current, minuscule form is more like a sapling than a redwood. Still he remains an important, if now more mischievous member, of the eclectic Guardians.

T9T4UG-209

GAMORA

A daughter of the evil Thanos, Gamora sought to escape her violent past and build a new life, free from her sins. When an unlikely twist of fate caused her to join the Guardians, the one-time *Most Dangerous Woman in The Galaxy* found her skills put to a better use – saving lives.

DRAX

Drax is a headstrong warrior whose reputation as *The Destroyer* is both feared and respected throughout the sector. Despite his menacing appearance, the fierce fighter's lust for battle conceals a warm heart. Though once scarred by the loss of his family, the peculiar Drax has found a new home with his equally eccentric allies in the *Guardians of the Galaxy*.

EGO

After decades apart, an unlikely twist of fate has reunited Peter Quill with his estranged father, Ego. Little is known of the secretive man, other than that he is a cosmic traveller with mysterious powers. What revelations does his arrival expose, and what will it mean for the *Guardians of the Galaxy*?

NEBULA

The second adopted daughter of the cosmic
tyrant Thanos, Nebula was genetically modified
with cybernetics to achieve victory by any means
necessary. Since her defeat at the hands of the
Guardians, Nebula comes hurtling back into the life
of her sister, Gamora, hoping to finally settle their
unfinished business. Now, Nebula will somewhat
reluctantly fight alongside the *Guardians of the
Galaxy*, whilst she contemplates her own capacity
for forgiveness.

MANTIS

A strange alien who serves Ego, Mantis slowly gets
to know the Guardians with the help of her special
powers. These abilities allow her to read the hidden
emotions at play within the group which make
for some embarrassing, hilarious and touching
moments. Mantis forms a special bond with Drax,
who teaches her about the universe and the
meaning of family from his own unique perspective.
Mantis becomes an important team member who
proves crucial to the Guardians over the course of
their advaneture.

word, her jaw hanging in disbelief that that no one had thought to see if she'd been sucked into space.

She watched Drax grab a cable from the wall and hook it to a loop on his belt. "Where are you going?" she demanded.

Drax smiled and said, "To meet with a worthy foe."

Over in the Sovereign pilot bay, all of the pilots had gathered around the lone pilot left chasing the Milano, cheering him on. Above, on the Observation Deck, High Priestess Ayesha motioned to the Admiral. "That pilot," she said, pointing down to where everyone was gathered, "tell me more about him."

"H-his name is Zylak," the Admiral stammered. "Top of his class. Laser focus. Killer instinct. Had to be disciplined once for being too aggressive."

Ayesha smiled. "Unleash him," she commanded.

Zylak heard the Admiral's command in his comm unit, and his lips curled into a vicious sneer. "Roger that," he replied. "Tell Her Highness I live to serve at her pleasure." He leaned forward and banked his Sovereign pod to the right, unleashing a barrage of laser blasts on the weaponless Milano. He had been impressed by the skills of the Milano pilot in the asteroid field, even though their evasion tactics had seemed erratic. Whoever was flying was gifted, there was no denying that. It was a shame he had to destroy them and make them pay for their crimes against the Sovereign.

Another stream of lasers hurtled toward the Milano. One found its mark on the other wing, blowing it apart on impact. Inside, each Guardian grabbed on to the closest secure thing they could find as the Milano went spinning into a brief spiral.

"Wingless AND weaponless. Anyone got any ideas?" Rocket asked.

"I am Groot?" the little tree suggested.

Rocket grinned at Groot's suggestion. "Sorry, pal," he said, "I don't think even Drax's mighty turds would be enough ammunition for this job."

In the back of the ship, Drax found a slot in the wall labelled "SPACESUITS FOR EMERGENCY". Under that, in Rocket's scribbled writing, were the words, "OR FOR FUN". He reached into the slot and pulled out a disc, which he slapped on the middle of his chest. Immediately, a shimmering gel-like sheath covered his entire body. His eyes lit up, and he grinned widely.

In the Sovereign pilot bay Zylak had a similar

glint in his eye as he readied himself for another pass. He unleashed a targeted blast, clipping the topside of the Milano. At this point, he was toying with them. Over his comm unit, he could hear his fellow pilots cheering him on. Okay, he thought, enough fun: time to execute the thieves. He directed his Sovereign pod up and around, positioning for his final approach.

In the flight deck of the Milano, Gamora eyed the radar display nervously. "Fifteen clicks," she said.

"Looks like he's coming around again," Rocket replied. "Hey, Drax, maybe you could throw your blades —" He stopped short and looked around. "Has anyone seen Drax?" he asked.

Meanwhile, wearing his shimmering spacesuit, Drax reached into another box bolted to the wall of the ship. Inside was a large, lethal-looking rifle.

"Do not even think of stealing. I do not like thieves," Drax said bluntly.

"Umm, have you looked at the people you hang out with?" Nebula said, pointing toward the flight deck.

Drax paused, then grunted. "They are exceptions," he said. "Now, goodbye."

"Goodbye?" Nebula repeated, before watching in shock as Drax exited through the backup shield, his own spacesuit momentarily merging with it before he floated out into space with his rifle.

In the flight deck, Gamora's eyes widened as she saw an image on her console. "I think I found Drax," she said, pointing out the side window at the huge warrior, who had his rifle aimed squarely at the approaching Sovereign pod.

Quill slowly banged his head against

the wall. "This cannot end well," he groaned. "Do other people have to deal with this level of crazy?"

On his screen, Zylak was shocked to see a small, grey object floating behind his target, connected by some kind of cable. As he got a closer look, he saw it had arms and legs. Scanning his data files, he realized it was one of the perpetrators: the Guardian they called Drax. Zylak chuckled. What a great opportunity for some target practice. Destroying the ship could wait a few more moments. He narrowed his targeting lasers on Drax and pulled the trigger.

The Milano suddenly jerked to the side, pulling the big warrior behind it. He barely seemed to notice how close he had come to being blown to pieces. Lifting his rifle, he took aim at the Sovereign pod and pulled the trigger.

"Die, spaceship," he said, smiling.

The laser from Drax's rifle found its

mark. Back in the Sovereign pilot bay, Zylak screamed as his ship blew up. He threw down his controls, defeated, and the other pilots parted to reveal High Priestess Ayesha watching from above. Her face was not happy. Zylak kneeled before her, but when he looked up again, she was gone.

"Five clicks!" Gamora exclaimed. They were almost about to make the jump.

"Perfect timing," Drax's voice boomed as he reappeared in the flight deck. "Once again, I have singlehandedly destroyed our foe!"

Quill considered correcting Drax, then thought better of it. "Nice shot, big guy. Alright, now it's time to…. Oh, no!"

Looking ahead out of the window, Quill felt his excitement immediately turn to despair. Dozens of Sovereign ships flew into formation between the Milano and the jump point.

In the Sovereign flight deck, Ayesha smiled faintly at the Admiral. "You have redeemed yourself," she said flatly. "Nicely done, Admiral."

Back on the Milano, Rocket looked at the Sovereign ships in disbelief. "How did they do that?" he asked, already grabbing his gun out of its holster. He was ready to go down fighting.

"They must have flown around the asteroid field," Quill answered. "Kind of like the tortoise and the hare thing."

Drax was confused. "Is Rocket the hare?" he asked.

"I'd teach you all about parables if we weren't about to die, Drax," Quill said.

"I am Groot." The other Guardians watched as Groot reached past them and tapped on a side window, directing their view to the space between the Milano and the Sovereign fleet: a sleek, oval-shaped floating ship had appeared seemingly out of nowhere.

"Yeah," Rocked nodded, "I've never seen a ship like that before either. Guys, you gotta see –"

Suddenly, a blinding burst of light cut off whatever Rocket was about to say. When the Guardians could see again, the entire Sovereign fleet was gone, apparently vaporized by the white light that appeared to have emanated from the strange floating vessel.

On the Sovereign flight deck, all was silent as the Admiral delivered the news of the fleet's destruction to Ayesha. She merely stood in place for several moments. The Admiral gulped. After a long pause, Ayesha turned to the Admiral.

"Who did this?" she asked, her voice growing louder with every word.

The Admiral bowed his head helplessly. Ayesha looked at the hundreds of now useless pilots standing below her, their heads also hung in shame. Without acknowledging them any further, she turned and marched out of the flight deck.

"Whoa – who did that?" Rocket whispered, not knowing he echoed Ayesha's own question.

Peter Quill didn't have the time to speculate. "Don't know, doesn't matter," he replied urgently. "There's the jump point. Go! Go! Go!"

The Milano's engines opened up and powered the battered ship as fast as they could towards the jump point.

"Hey, Quill!" Rocket called, still staring at the mysterious ship outside. "I think you're gonna want to come take a look at this."

There, standing on the edge of the oval-shaped ship, was the outline of a man. He seemed ... relaxed, yet powerful, as if the obliteration of an entire Sovereign fleet was something he saw every day.

Quill caught a glimpse of the man as the Milano rapidly approached the jump point. He couldn't be entirely sure, but it seemed as though the man was staring right back at him, raising his hand in a casual wave just as the Milano disappeared into the space jump.

Chapter 07

"Okay, everybody," Peter Quill warned, "prepare yourselves for a really bad –"

He was cut off as the Milano smashed through a forest, flattening trees, splitting branches, and mowing through the underbrush. Looking around, he saw that everyone was safely strapped in, braced for impact – except for Groot, who was munching on sweets as though they were popcorn and he was watching a movie.

"I am Groot!" he shouted, excitedly, eyes wide open.

With a loud THUD, the Milano broke through and landed on the cool surface of the planet Berhert, leaving a path of dirt and flattened brush behind it. Quill winced as he saw a mass of leaves and branches pressed against the window.

As everyone else tried to unbuckle their straps and get their bearings, Drax remained seated, breathing in excitedly as if he'd just been on a roller-coaster adventure. "That was amazing," he said, smiling.

Gamora rolled her eyes at him before turning her glare towards Rocket and Quill. "We could have died. Because of your arrogance," she yelled, exasperated.

Peter raised his hands defensively and turned towards Rocket. "More like because he stole the Anulax batteries," he protested.

"You know why I did it, Star-Munch?" Rocket shot back. Quill crossed his arms ignoring him. "Do you?" Rocket asked again.

"I'm not going to answer to 'Star-Munch'," Peter retorted.

Rocket got in Quill's face. "I did it because I wanted to," he hissed. "And we would have escaped just fine if you could fly more like me and less like the Ravagers you grew up with."

"Jerk," Peter muttered.

"Thankfully, that tiny man on the ship saved us by blowing up an entire army with a blast of light," Rocket said, settling back in his chair.

"How tiny?" Drax asked.

Rocket demonstrated with his thumb and forefinger. "Like this."

"A three-centimetre-tall man saved us?" Gamora snorted.

"Well, if he got closer, I'm sure he'd be bigger," Rocket continued.

"That's how sight works, you silly raccoon!" Quill yelled, losing his patience.

"Don't call me a raccoon!" Rocket yelled.

"Oh, I'm sorry," Peter said in an overly-exaggerated apologetic voice, "I meant to say 'trash panda'!"

Rocket opened his mouth to respond, but Quill's insult seemed to have caught him off-guard. Turning to Drax, he asked, "Is that better or worse?"

"I don't know," Drax replied with a shrug.

Quill turned to Drax, laughing. "It's much worse."

Now Rocket was ready to respond. "You smelly, hairless –" he started to shout while lunging at Quill, when Groot suddenly jumped between the two, pointing up.

"I am Groot! I am Groot!" he repeated excitedly.

Quill and Rocket stopped and looked in the direction Groot was pointing. It couldn't be. The Guardians quickly ran to the back of the ship, now torn completely open, where Nebula was casually pointing up to the sky. "Someone followed you through the jump point," she said.

As the dust began to swirl around them, the Guardians drew their weapons, everyone standing back-to-back, ready to attack – or defend. Nebula tried to join them, but she was still chained to the Milano.

"Set me free," Nebula hissed at her sister. "You'll need my help."

Gamora scoffed at the suggestion. "I'm not a fool, Nebula," she responded.

"You're a fool if you leave one of your best hand-to-hand combatants chained up during a fight," Nebula shot back, shaking her bonds at Gamora.

"You'll attack me the moment I let you go," Gamora countered.

"No, I won't," Nebula said, rather unconvincingly.

Quill, standing next to the bickering sisters, chimed in, "You'd think an evil super villain would learn how to lie better." Just then the ship Nebula had pointed out – the same oval-shaped ship that had helped them escape the Sovereign fleet – landed, crushing all of the trees around it.

Drax's eyes lit up. "I bet it's the three-centimetre man!" he said hopefully.

With a hisssss as the ship's cabin decompressed and a jet of steam came pouring out, a hatch opened. The outline of a man could be seen striding down. Although he had no recollection of ever seeing something or someone like this, Quill felt his stomach knot up. Something about this stranger felt familiar, like some kind of distant, faded memory. But why? All he could do was wait and find out.

Behind the mysterious man was a strange-but-beautiful woman with antennae. She looked at everyone in the group, one by one. The man's eyes, however, never left Peter.

He burst into a charming smile.

"After all these years," he said, extending his arms towards Quill, "I've found you. I never thought I'd see you again, Peter."

Quill stood stiff, still ready to use his weapons if it came to that. "Thanks for the assist back there," he said, his voice defiant, "but who are you? And how do you know my name?"

The man's roguish smile grew even larger as he strode closer, a familiar swagger to his walk. "I figured my rugged good looks would make it obvious to you, even after thirty years. My name's Ego," he continued, "and I'm your dad, Peter."

Peter Quill's weapon and jaw dropped at the same time.

Chapter 08

Despite its two overlapping suns, the planet Contraxia was as bitterly cold as the souls who dared visit its most infamous bar, The Iron Lotus. Located in a frenzied town of flashy buildings and neon lights, The Iron Lotus served a primary clientele of Ravagers.

The Ravagers were like an underground brotherhood – some might call them space-pirates – dedicated to finding (or stealing, if necessary) objects of value throughout the galaxy and delivering them to the highest bidder. These objects weren't always considered 'legal', but for Yondu Udonta, a job was a job. But even the Ravagers abided by certain unspoken codes and

Yondu's "a job is a job" approach sometimes crossed the line. His reputation was growing among the Ravagers, and not in a good way.

Yondu quietly exited his suite at The Iron Lotus and glanced over at an older Ravager, Tullk, who nodded back to him. They were immediately flanked by two bodyguards. Together, they entered the main barroom of The Iron Lotus, where the sound of a familiar voice stopped Yondu in his tracks.

Swearing under his breath, Yondu scanned the room. A group of Ravagers in blue uniforms were seated around a table. One of them appeared to be made of diamonds. Yondu had heard of this one. Martinex, they called him. The voice Yondu had recognized came from a man named Stakar, a legend among the Ravagers. When he spoke, Ravagers often followed. It was best to either be on his good side or not on his radar at all. Unfortunately, Yondu was neither.

Stakar was in the middle of a boisterous tale. "And I was like, Aleta, I love you, but you're crazy, you have always been crazy –"

Just then, Martinex spotted Yondu and nodded at Stakar. Yondu had no choice. He decided the best course of action was to face Stakar like a man. A terrified man, but a man, nonetheless.

"Stakar," Yondu said, as confidently as he could manage. "Been some time. I'd –"

Stakar stood and stared Yondu down until the blue-skinned Ravager fell into a seat. "Seems like this establishment is the wrong kind of disreputable," he growled. There was venom in his voice.

"Stakar...." Yondu began to plead.

The grizzled Ravager ignored him and instead spoke in the direction of The Iron Lotus's owner, a Sneeper. "There are a hundred Ravager factions," he called. "You just lost the business of ninety-nine by serving one."

"Please, sir," the owner begged from behind the counter. "Please!"

Yondu watched as Stakar and the rest of his gang, along with everyone else in the room, emptied the saloon. In short order, the only people left were Yondu and the rest of his crew, including a man named Kraglin, Yondu's right hand. They all looked to Yondu expectantly. His jaw set, Yondu jumped up out of the seat, his jaw set in grim determination, and marched out after Stakar.

In the freezing wind and snow, Yondu called out to Stakar, "You know what? I don't care what you think of me!"

"Then why are you following us?" Stakar asked, turning to face Yondu, fists clenched.

"'Cause you'll listen to what I gotta say," Yondu spat back, his own arms braced in defensive posture, in case it came to that.

"I don't got to listen to nothing!" Stakar scoffed. "You betrayed the code. Ravagers don't deal in —"

"I didn't know what the cargo was!" Yondu interrupted. "All I knew is someone was paying a pretty penny for it!"

"Don't lie to my face, Yondu," Stakar sneered. He leaned in towards Yondu, who flinched slightly. "You didn't know 'cause you chose not to know, 'cause it made you rich!"

The Ravager turned to walk away, but his point was clearly lost on Yondu, who pleaded, "I demand a seat at the table! I wear the flames, same as you!"

Stakar hesitated, his shoulders dropping briefly. The battle-worn Ravager had seen others banished — but he, himself, had never done it. For a Ravager, it was a punishment almost worse than death. But he knew it must be done. Squaring his shoulders again, he turned back to face Yondu.

"Yondu Udonta," he began, "you may dress like a Ravager, but you won't hear no Horns of Freedom when you die and the colours of Ogord will NOT flash over your grave. You think I take some pleasure in exiling you? You're wrong. You broke all our hearts. May our paths never cross again."

With that, Stakar and the others stormed off into the snowy night. Martinex stayed behind for a brief moment, studying Yondu silently, then turned to follow the others, glints of light flashing off his diamond skin.

Standing outside The Iron Lotus alone, Yondu felt the snow fall gently on his skin as the only way of life he'd ever known was ripped away from him.

Behind him, Yondu's crew huddled closer together. They saw their leader stripped of his status, wondering what that might mean for them. Either way, the murmurs of mutiny began to spread among the group.

"First Quill betrays us and Yondu just lets him go scot-free," whispered a monstrously large Ravager named Taserface. "Now he's gettin' all riled over nothing. We followed him 'cause he was the one who wasn't afraid to do what needed to be done." He gestured at the crushed-looking Yondu, standing alone in the snow. "Seems like he's going soft."

"If he's so soft, why you whispering for," challenged Kraglin.

Taserface stared Kraglin dead in the eyes. Without blinking, he said, "You know I'm right, Kraglin."

Tullk stepped in between the two men and warned, "You'd best watch what you say about the Cap'n, Tay –"

He was stopped mid-sentence by a sleek vessel landing in front of The Iron Lotus. As the doors opened, two Sovereign chambermaids rolled out a long, blue cloth that stopped exactly at Yondu's feet. High Priestess Ayesha passed by the crew of Ravagers, ignoring them. Stopping at the end of the blue cloth, she forced a smile. So soft was her walk that Yondu hadn't heard her.

"Yondu Udonta," she said, her voice startling him as he turned to face her. "I have a proposition for you."

As white snow fell on his blue skin, Yondu considered his options. Seeing as he was no longer a Ravager, he didn't have many left. With his signature smirk, he cocked his head slightly, all ears.

Chapter 09

Ever since Peter Quill had learned he was only half human, he had wondered what the other half was. Would he suddenly sprout wings one day? Turn blue and grow gills to swim under water? The possibilities had seemed endless. Instead, looking at Ego eating heartily across the campfire, he realized his other half was just … this man. Apparently an incredibly powerful man who wiped out fleets of spaceships for fun – but still, just a man. Part of Peter was relieved, but mostly, after all these years, he was filled with questions.

"Why?" he asked bluntly.

Ego didn't need the question to be

expanded. He knew where his son was coming from.

"Your mother was dying," he replied, "so I hired Yondu to pick you up."

"Maybe you should check babysitter references," Quill muttered under his breath.

"I would have come for you myself," Ego continued, "but I was in the midst of an intergalactic battle against demonic forces and trying to save this dimension. I think. They all start to bleed together." He tried to explain as best he could. "Yondu was supposed to return you, but he kept you for himself. I have no idea why."

Quill scoffed, recalling his younger days. "Because I was a skinny kid who could squeeze into places adults couldn't," he said. "Easier for thieving."

"Believe me, my son, I've been trying to find you ever since," Ego entreated, true remorse in his eyes.

"I thought Yondu was your father?" Drax piped in, slightly confused.

"WHAT?!" Quill was amazed at how dense his teammate could be sometimes.

"You look exactly alike," Drax muttered in defence.

Rocket rolled his eyes and laughed. "One's blue!" he said.

Even Groot looked at Drax in disbelief. "I am Groot," he said, shaking his head.

"Yondu wasn't a father," Quill said, speaking almost to himself. "He was the guy who abducted me, taught me how to fight, and kept me in constant terror by threatening to eat me!" He was getting completely worked up just at the memories.

"Eat you?!" Ego exclaimed in horror. His eyes narrowed. "That low-down, dirty –"

Gamora interrupted. "After all this time,

how did you locate us now?" she asked, a slight suspicion in her voice.

Ego stood, proudly looking at his son. "Even where I reside," he began, "out past the edge of what is known, we've heard tell of the man they call Star-Lord."

Quill's chest puffed up with pride. "Ha! See? Told ya," he said, before noticing that no one was impressed. He turned his attention back to his father, who was still looking only at him.

"What do you say we head there now?" Ego asked.

"Past the edge of what is known?" Gamora asked, eyebrow raised.

Ego continued to address Quill directly. "You and the rest of your associates are welcome," he said, "even the triangle-faced monkey there. I promise you, it's like nothing you've ever seen before." Ego paused, then continued softly, "And there, I can explain your very special heritage in much more detail. Everything will be made perfectly clear."

Quill stared at Ego. The father-son trip he'd longed for since he was a child was actually going to become a reality. The answers he'd longed for all his life were a hyper-jump away. So why wouldn't his mouth open and yell, "Of course! Let's go!"?

A light touch on his arm broke his daydream. It was Gamora. "Peter, we need to go for a walk," she said.

Ego stretched his arms, realizing his father-son moment had been interrupted. "And I need to go to the bathroom," he quipped. "Everybody needs something around here."

Whistling, Ego walked off into the bushes as Gamora and Peter headed in the other direction, behind the Milano. Groot, Rocket and Drax remained by the campfire with the woman who had come off the spaceship with Ego. Her name, they had learned, was Mantis. After a few moments of silence, Drax looked at Mantis, who was staring back at him, her mouth stretched into a creepy, too-wide smile.

"What are you doing?" Drax asked, unnerved and worried.

"Smiling," Mantis said, without changing her expression. "I have heard it is the thing to do to make people like you."

Drax shook his head and said, "Not if you do it like that."

Mantis dropped her exaggerated smile. "Oh," she said, slightly embarrassed. "I was raised alone on Ego's planet. I do not understand the complexities of social interaction."

"I am an excellent teacher. You may follow what I do and learn much from me," Drax offered helpfully.

Rocket was busy checking one of his weapons, paying no attention to Drax or Mantis.

"Of course Quill's dad would be named 'Ego'," he muttered. "All makes sense now."

Pointing at Rocket, Mantis gave a slight grin of excitement. "Can I pet your puppy?" she asked Drax. "It is adorable!"

Drax looked over at the unaware Rocket, a mischievous grin crossing his face. "Yes," he said, "he loves to be scratched behind the ears."

Mantis moved towards Rocket, reaching out to rub him behind his ears. Rocket spotted movement out of the corner of his eye and immediately turned and snapped, almost biting Mantis's hand.

Mantis pulled back her hand and scooted back to Drax, giggling nervously. Drax was laughing heartily.

"That," he said, "is what we call a practical joke!"

She looked at Drax, joy in her eyes. "I

liked it very much!" she exclaimed.

Drax smiled at Mantis in appreciation. He could get along well with her.

In a clearing behind the Milano, Gamora found herself trying to convince Quill of the dangers of following the man claiming to be his father into the unknown reaches of the galaxy, but his mind seemed made up.

"We have no reason to believe he's actually your father," Gamora said as patiently as possible. "This feels like an easy trap. Kree purists, the Ravagers, now the Sovereign – who could have easily tracked us. They all want us dead."

Peter pointed in the direction of Ego. "Not him," he said. "He saved our lives."

Gamora sighed in exasperation, but continued, "We saved Nebula's – for the bounty. Who says he isn't doing the same? Or for any other reason we can't see yet?"

"Look," Quill said, "when I was a kid, I'd carry around a picture of this guy I told people was my dad. It was David Hasselhoff."

Gamora stared at him blankly. "Who is that?"

"A super-cool guy who was a singer and an actor on a show where his car talked," Quill explained.

"Why did it talk?" Gamora asked, confused.

"To fight crime and be a good pal," Quill shrugged.

Gamora didn't understand what a talking car had to do with anything, but she sensed Quill was opening up to her. "That's really sweet, Peter," she said, reaching out to touch Quill's hand before he pulled it away, "but –"

"– no, it's sad," he countered. "Everyone knew that wasn't my real dad. I'd see all the other kids with their dads ... All I wanted, more than anything, was to have my own father. What if this is my chance? What if he's a total Hasselhoff?" Quill's voice broke slightly.

"It is unlikely he is a Hasselhoff," Gamora said plainly.

"But who says we shouldn't check out who he really is?" Quill asked, his eyes full of longing. Gamora knew there was no talking him out of this. She gave a very slight nod, then turned and walked back towards the campfire. Quill did a tiny fist pump behind her. His dream was coming true. Or so he hoped.

Moments later, inside the Milano, Gamora was packing up their gear while her sister screamed, "You're leaving me with that fox?!" Nebula was incensed.

Rocket threw down a spanner, reached for a blaster, and said, "How many times do I have to say it? NOT. A. FOX!"

"Shoot her if she does anything suspicious," Gamora instructed, glancing at Nebula. "Or if you feel like it. Just keep her alive." Rocket grunted in disappointment at that last part.

A small voice spoke up behind Gamora. "I am Groot." The young sapling looked as if he were about to cry.

Gamora picked him up gently. "It will just be a couple days," she explained. "We'll be back before Rocket's finished fixing the ship."

She set him back down, and he went over to Rocket, ready to cry on his shoulder. "Watch it – you know I hate getting wet," Rocket said in his own consoling way. "We've been alone before, pal. This is nothing."

The group gathered outside Ego's ship, where he was waiting to welcome them. "I'm glad you've decided to take this trip," he said to Quill. "Hopefully it's the first step in making things up to you." Ego patted his son's shoulder and entered the ship with Mantis.

Drax, Gamora and Quill looked back at the Guardians they were leaving behind. "Don't break my ship any more than it is, fuzzy!" Quill called out to Rocket.

"Hope your daddy isn't as big of a jerk as you, orphan boy," Rocket shot back.

Quill smiled. Drax and Gamora entered the ship, but he hesitated and took one last look at the Milano. Groot was waving goodbye wildly. Quill felt that familiar sense of nerves and adrenaline rise in his chest as he turned to enter Ego's ship. His first father-son adventure, his childhood dream, was about to begin.

Chapter 10

The firelight crackled as all four moons of Berhert hit their zenith, casting a light-blue glow. Inside the Milano, Rocket hummed along to a catchy tune from Quill's Awesome Mix Vol. 2, absentmindedly chewing on a cut piece of wire as he examined the damage caused by the fight with the Sovereign fleet and the crash-landing (none of which was his fault, of course).

"Hey, you – Fox. Do you have any actual food lying around this garbage heap?" Nebula asked grumpily.

"I'm not talking to you until you stop calling me names," Rocket shot back.

"What name did I call you?" Nebula

asked, genuinely confused and increasingly annoyed with Rocket.

"I am Groot," said a small voice, the little Guardian shaking a branch at her as though she should know better.

"Exactly," Rocket agreed, nodding his head and going back to work.

"Exactly what? I don't speak tiny-tree language," Nebula snarled.

"Well, talking to my friend with that attitude isn't going to do you any favours." Rocket winked and gave Groot a high five.

Nebula rattled her chains, fed up with the two of them. "Can't you go forage for some food in the forest?" she demanded. "How are you the one in charge of fixing the spaceship, anyway? No wonder it looks like a child built it!"

"Just for that, no foraged food for Miss Cranky Pants. Got it, Groot?" Rocket responded.

Groot smiled. "I am Groot," he said

with a salute.

"Oh, but can ya be a pal and bring me a bit of that Xandarian-cured meat I know Drax keeps hidden under his bunk?" Rocket asked, winking at Nebula. "All this hard work – I'm starving!"

"I'll roast you over this fire like the rodent you are," Nebula growled.

"Oooooo, I'm shaking in my boots," Rocket whimpered. Then he became more serious and approached Nebula. "Look, we're both thieves, right? Theoretically, we SHOULD like each other, or have a little honour. Problem is, every time I've seen you, you wanna kill me or one of my friends. Too bad, 'cuz I can be a pretty good pal. But try and come for me, even out here? I'll always get the first shot, even if my guns are holstered." Rocket was menacingly close to Nebula now. Suddenly his face dropped back into a smile as Groot tossed him the meat.

"Time to feast like a king! Glad we came to this understanding. I feel the air is cleared – do you feel the air is clearer, pal?"

"I am Groot," his companion said with a mouth full of meat.

Nebula gave him a sinister glare and began plotting in her mind the different ways she'd kill Rocket as soon as she was free. She slumped back against the ship and looked into the sky as Rocket started humming again, now adding a little dance to his step.

Deep in the woods towering over the Milano, Rocket was unaware of menacing eyes peering down on him. Taserface, the monstrous Ravager, and Kraglin, Yondu's right hand, quietly crested a hilltop to get a better view of the grounded ship and its occupants.

"Finally," Taserface growled, "our chance to get some real vengeance on Quill and his gnats."

"I'm sure Yondu –" Kraglin started, before being interrupted by a sneer from the huge Ravager.

"Sure Yondu what, Kraglin? 'Cuz I think he's just playing lapdog to that gold lady. He may be the hired gun, but only someone with power like hers could get us THIS." Taserface swept his arm behind him. Descending into the valley were dozens of M-ships landing softly on the other side of the ridge from the Milano. Within moments there were squads of Ravagers pouring out from each ship, all moving to the top of the hill. Standing in the centre, like a king who'd finally reclaimed his throne, was Yondu. Aware of all the eyes on him, he took a moment to savour the sweet turn fortune had given him.

Yondu looked over at Kraglin a few metres away and nodded at his trusted ally. Turning back to the troops, he waved his hand for them to follow, swiftly but quietly.

"Don't forget it was Yondu she hired, not you, Taserface," Kraglin warned. Taserface scoffed and marched along with the rest of the Ravagers.

As the Ravagers began to circle the Milano, Taserface's adrenaline rose. He was ready to attack! He could hear Rocket humming a soft, upbeat dance hit in the small radius cast by the lights on in the Milano. He couldn't wait any longer. He glanced at the Ravager next to him, who looked wild-eyed and completely unhinged, and gave a big thumbs-up. Then they both crashed through the brush and began to run towards the Milano. But Taserface couldn't keep up. Nor could he warn his fellow Ravager when he heard a CLICK as he stomped right onto a trap buried in the underbrush.

Taserface quickly hit the ground and yelled, "Trap!" His warning was too late, however, as almost a hundred darts suddenly shot from the treetops directly at the Ravagers. As the darts hit their marks, the Ravagers fell by the dozens. The Ravager who'd set off the trap was still standing there, looking around in amazement and confusion. Before he could take another step, though, a blast rang out through the forest, and he fell to the ground.

The sound of the shot woke Nebula with a jolt deep inside the Milano. She could still hear Rocket humming, but in an odd, repetitive way. Just then, she noticed he had taped his walkie-talkie to the open window and pointed it outwards so the speakers faced the woods. "Idiot WANTS us to get killed," Nebula muttered, shaking her head and looking at Groot, who was cowering in the corner.

"I am Groot," he said, genuinely afraid Rocket may have got them in over their heads this time.

Rocket slung his rifle over his shoulder

and pulled out a remote detonator with two buttons on it. One was labelled "BANG", the other, "BIGGER BANG". Crouched in a tree above the Milano and still humming his song into his comm, Rocket extended the antennae of the detonator and watched as two different Ravager squadrons drew closer and closer. With a gleam in his eye, Rocket pressed the "BANG" button. One entire squadron flew into the air as an electro-current blast shot through them. The other squadron stopped in its tracks. Perfect place, Rocket thought with a grin. The "BIGGER BANG" button lived up to its name as the squadron – and part of a nearby tree – suffered the same electro-current blast as their accomplices.

Rocket's giggles interrupted his humming on the radio, and one of the Ravagers spotted him. "There!" shouted the Ravager, but it was too late. Rocket propelled himself from one tree branch to another and began pushing buttons in alternative sequences, making Ravager after Ravager fly up into the air until the electro-current concussive blasts ran out of energy.

Back on the Milano, Nebula tried her best to plead with Groot, but it wasn't working. "Your friend, the furry one, he's in serious danger," she said. "He needs my help." She held out her shackles. "Please, let me go join him."

Groot looked at her very suspiciously. "I am Groot?"

Nebula sighed. "If you're talking about when I said I'd fry him, I take it back, okay?" she bargained sweetly, but Groot did not look convinced. The sound of Rocket jumping and grunting as he leapt from branch to branch gave Nebula an idea. "Look, Groot, just hand me that comm unit. I think I have an idea." Groot was used to hearing his fellow Guardians say those words and they almost always ended up leaving them in worse situations. But what's the worst she could do with a comm unit, he wondered.

Several metres outside, Rocket was crouched quietly in a tree as half a dozen Ravagers made their way through the forest looking for him. Rocket held his breath and waited – and waited – until the last one passed. Smiling, Rocket dropped down onto the shoulder of the last man in the squadron and took out a handful of small, sticky discs. He slapped one on the man's back and then leaped forward, slapping another on the shoulder blades of the man directly in front of him, and then leaped again, and so on until he reached the front of the squadron. All the Ravagers were wildly flailing about trying to reach for the discs, but they couldn't grasp them.

"Here ya go, fellas. Lemme get those for ya," Rocket said as he pulled out a small device with a switch. Jumping high into the air, he flipped the switch; the Ravagers all began to convulse as electricity flowed through the discs. They flopped around and then fell all at once.

Rocket was so busy laughing, he didn't notice a bulky Ravager named Brahl and his tough compatriot sneaking up on him from opposite sides.

"Ain't so tough now without your little toys, are ya?" Brahl taunted.

"Who needs toys when I can just borrow yours?" Rocket asked. "I'll just kick you in the face and have your friend shoot you. Wanna see? It's pretty cool." Rocket crouched low as he spoke.

Without warning, Rocket leaped into the air, punching Brahl in the throat. The other Ravager fired, but Rocket back-flipped out of the way, and the blast hit Brahl, instead. Rocket landed on the second Ravager's head and rapid-punched until both Ravagers were lying unconscious, Rocket standing between them.

"See? I told ya. No toys, and I still —" Rocket gloated, before being cut off by the eerily familiar sound of a high-pitched whistle slicing through the night air. He looked up just in time to see Yondu's arrow streaking down, straight toward him.

Rocket cried out, bracing himself. But another whistle caused the arrow to stop suddenly, suspended just in front of Rocket's forehead.

"Hey there, rat," came the gravelly voice of Yondu Udonta as he walked out of the forest, a large smile on his face. "Aren't you glad to see me?"

Chapter 11

Nebula signalled to a trembling Groot to stay quiet and still as the unlikely duo huddled in their hiding place within the Milano. They watched as the Ravagers, led by Yondu, marched Rocket towards the ship, an arrow floating dangerously close to the Guardian's head.

"Any minute now, baby tree," she whispered. "I hope," she muttered under her breath to herself.

As Rocket was being led to the Milano, he tried to engage his captors in conversation while he thought of his next move.

"So, Yondu, how's life been, ya big blue idiot?" he asked as casually as possible.

"Not so bad," Yondu chuckled back, knowing he had Rocket trapped and was on his way to accomplishing his mission. He'd love to see Stakar turn him away from a seat at the table now! "We got a pretty good gig. A golden gal with quite a high opinion of herself."

"You two must get along great," Rocket sneered, thinking back to his last interaction with High Priestess Ayesha.

"Ha," Yondu laughed. "Too uptight for me, but the money she offered up for you and your pals will do just fine. Sounds like you got on the wrong side of her radar. As usual. Luckily, she was able to show me your last known location. The jump point was pretty easy to figure out after that – I just looked for the most hospitable planet nearby, knowing how much you mucked up your ship here."

Yondu nodded to the damaged Milano.

Kraglin leaned in to Yondu and asked, "What about the tracer we put on the hull during the War over Xandar?"

"That was a backup," Yondu growled. "I got us here, didn't I?"

"Yes, boss," Kraglin said, nodding meekly.

"And I captured the rodent, didn't I?" Yondu asked, louder this time, addressing the larger group.

A half-hearted chorus of "Yeah"s, "Sure thing, Capt'n"s, and "Uh huh"s came from the dozen or so remaining Ravagers.

"So this gold chick, she's paying you to kill us?" Rocket asked, a plan forming in his head.

"Plus a bonus if we return the stolen batteries," Yondu answered.

Rocket turned quickly to face his captors. "You give your word you won't hurt Groot an' me, and I'll tell you where the batteries are," he said.

Yondu grinned, his craggy teeth shining. "Lucky for you my word don't mean squat. If it did, I'd actually hand you over to that lady. Money talks, fur-ball."

Taserface stood erect to his monstrous height. "You're just gonna let them go?" he demanded. "That woman offered us a million for the batteries PLUS whatever we can get for their corpses!"

"Who's the captain around here?" Yondu responded, his voice steady with authority. "Besides, we can get more for the batteries individually than what she's offerin'. And we can fake some dead bodies to look like Quill and the rest."

As Yondu was speaking, Rocket noticed something in the forest behind the Ravagers, a movement so subtle that the branches barely shook. Suddenly he was filled with hope. All he had to do was keep the Ravagers distracted.

"I'm with Yondu on this one," Rocket chimed in. "All you need is any fried, furry thing and…." He spun around, fell on the ground, stuck his tongue out, and played dead.

"Get up, you idiot," Yondu said, prodding him with his boot.

Without moving, his eyes squinted shut, Rocket muttered out of the corner of his mouth, "Can't … move … I'm dead…."

Yondu sighed and said, "Look, we're on a timetable, and it doesn't include your little theatre in the park. So be a good pet and get me those batteries, and we'll be on our way."

Taserface reached for his weapon. "Like hell," he snarled. "Not without their corpses, too. I think you've gone a little soft, Yondu – maybe it's time for new leadership."

Yondu's blue face flushed as he saw the mutiny unfolding before him. "We're not stupid enough to actually KILL the Guardians of the

Galaxy!" he fumed. "We'd have the whole Nova Corps on us."

Another tough-looking Ravager drew his weapon, as well. "Maybe with the right one in charge, we could handle them," he said.

Sensing the support growing for him, the monstrous Taserface widened his mouth into a terrifying grin, showing two rows of teeth. "I don't give a spit about the Nova Corps," he snarled, "but you sure seem to be worried about a lot of things these days. Not focused on doin' yer job as a leader." Turning his back on Yondu, he addressed the other Ravagers, his voice booming: "Who's with me in stripping the flames once and for all off Yondu like Stakar said?"

A resounding chorus of "Aye"s roared through the forest.

Yondu seethed in anger at this sudden betrayal. "You wouldn't dare," he sneered. "None of ya know the ways this galaxy operates.

None of ya are fit ta lead!" Turning to the only person he thought he could trust, Yondu felt almost desperate. "Tell 'em I'm right, Kraglin," he said, his voice cracking.

Kraglin could only kick the dirt, his eyes not meeting his leader's. "I-I'm not sure, Yondu," he said haltingly. "Maybe it's best we let someone new try. Just for a little bit."

"Someone new?!" Yondu roared. "Like who, for instance?"

"I nominate me," Taserface growled.

In a flash, the large Ravager had Yondu's hands cuffed in chains. He was so close Yondu could smell the rations Taserface had been eating earlier.

The other Ravagers began to chant, "Taserface! Captain! Taserface!" He stood to his full height, looking down at Yondu, whose world was crumbling before his eyes.

"Now kneel," the mutineer bellowed,

prompting a chorus of derisive laughter among the Ravagers. Yondu didn't move. Never in his decades of travels with the Ravagers did he imagine he'd face such a mutiny.

At his feet, Yondu heard a sharp whisper. "Hey, Boy Blue." It was Rocket. "Maybe it's a good idea ta do what he says. Like, right about now."

Yondu looked fiercely at Rocket. "You with them too?" he hissed. "I ain't kneeling ta nobody."

Rocket shrugged. "Your death," he said. "But don't say I never tried to help you out." Yondu simply glared at him in response.

Rocket looked nervously at the trees. No movement. Turning his attention back to the mounting tension, he waved his hands in the air. "Hold on!" he shouted up at Taserface. The other Ravagers all hushed and started coming at him. "There's got to be some sort of peaceful resolution here! Or even a violent resolution, where I'm standing over THERE!"

Suddenly, as if on cue, two blasts rang out. Rocket looked down at his body – he was still in one piece. The blasts had knocked the guns from the Ravagers' hands. Everyone looked around. A voice in the darkness came from the trees.

"NOT killing the Guardians is the smartest thing I think I've ever heard you say, Yondu." At that moment a light began to radiate, illuminating the tree line. It revealed the white ship belonging to Ego. Star-Lord, blasters drawn, was standing on top of it. The hatch opened, and Gamora and Drax rushed out, ready for battle.

A handful of Ravagers turned towards the Guardians and rushed to attack, Taserface leading the way. Drax and Gamora met them head on. Drax's blades and Gamora's sword whirled in a blur as the pair of Guardians quickly disarmed the Ravagers. Drax took particular pleasure in knocking Taserface out cold. Rocket couldn't let them have all the fun. He sprang onto a Ravager's back, scrambling up and down the Ravager, biting his ears and punching him until he eventually fell to the ground, a clawed mess.

"THAT'S for not staying down earlier!" Rocket said, wiping his hands clean on his uniform.

Smiling nervously, Yondu stepped forward. "Quill, my boy," he said. "Good to see you. Your little friend and I were just closing a deal to make sure –"

Star-Lord backed away from the blue-skinned Ravager. "Not so fast," he said. "There's someone here who'd probably like to say a thing or two to you. Remember how you were supposed to raise me all safe and sound? Yeah, about that...."

"We had a deal, Yondu," came a voice

from inside the ship. Yondu paled at the sound of it, knowing the speaker before Ego emerged, eyes narrowed.

"N-never thought I'd see you again," Yondu stammered.

"No, you were too busy recruiting my son into a life of thievery and debauchery," Ego said. "But it is all in the past. What's done is done." Ego glanced at his son and continued, "We have bigger things to take care of," without giving any further details.

"Well, if ya don't mind, looks like you folks have some catching up to do, so why don't we just part ways here?" Yondu said.

Ego shrugged, and turned to leave, but Quill nudged him. "Can we at least do something about that?" he asked, pointing to the handcuffs on Yondu's wrists. "I mean, he's not perfect, but he did raise me like his own son."

Ego's eyes flicked over Yondu, then took

in the crowd of mutinous Ravagers standing further back. "I do believe we have one more bit of business," he said.

A small beam of light streamed from Ego's fingertip. Yondu closed his eyes and braced himself. Then, he heard a clink at his feet. Looking down, he saw the cuffs that bound him had fallen off.

The other Ravagers huddled nervously. "What are you gonna do to us?" Kraglin asked, his voice shaking.

"You will not be taking any prisoners back to the Sovereign," Ego said to Kraglin. "You will follow the orders of your rightful Captain, Yondu."

"Y-yes, yes, sir," Kraglin stammered.

"That's right," Yondu shouted, his confidence rising again now that the mutiny had been quelled. He walked to where Taserface still lay unconscious and firmly placed the cuffs that once held him on the mutineer's arms. "And we got a lotta talking to do," he growled.

"Remember, stay away from Ayesha and the rest of the Sovereign," Quill warned. "As far as they know, you never found us!"

Yondu gave Quill a thumbs-up and winked. "You got it, my boy!" he replied with a wave.

The Ravagers hurried away, boarded their ships, and took off. Rocket watched them go and let out a big sigh of relief. "Well, THAT went exceedingly not the way I had planned. Not that I mind the assist, Quill, but how in the world did you know to –"

Gamora held up a walkie-talkie. Rocket, looking confused, said, "But I wasn't on your channel?"

"Ahem," came a voice from behind. Rocket turned to see Nebula holding another walkie-talkie, Groot standing beside her.

"I am Groot!" said Groot with a grin.

"Your tiny tree wouldn't unshackle me to help fight," Nebula explained, "so I took a chance that your friends might still be in range." She paused and waited for some sort of thanks.

Rocket gave Groot a big hug and said, "Great thinking, pal!"

Nebula sighed and tossed the walkie-talkie away.

"My sister's gambit paid off. For that, I suppose some gratitude is in order," Gamora said reluctantly. "You're still being turned in for ransom when we return."

"I feel so loved," Nebula sneered and walked back into the Milano.

Quill clapped his hands together to get everyone's attention. "Okay, warm and fuzzies all taken care of? Great. As far as the Sovereign know, we're lost, and the Ravagers are … well, as competent as Ravagers can be." He rolled his eyes before continuing, "But for now, I think we should stick together as a team, in case we encounter any more little surprises. Rocket and Groot, you're coming with us. My dad wants to fly us off on some secret mission at the edge of the universe – which sounds totally awesome."

Groot jumped up and boarded Ego's ship, cheering, "I am Groot!" Gamora and Drax checked Nebula's shackles, then turned to follow Groot onto the ship. Quill was about to join them, but Rocket held him back for a moment. "Hey, uh, Quill, thanks for coming back and not screwing up saving us," he said. "You're full of surprises, I guess."

Quill turned to look at his teammate. "Those two sisters may hate each other, but we're the Guardians of the Galaxy, man. We gotta look out for each other," he said, smiling. "Nobody else is."

With that, the two Guardians entered

Ego's ship, the hatch closed, and they took off, once again leaving for parts unknown. Watching the forest disappear below them, Rocket knew that even if the Guardians had no idea where they were going next, his friends would have his back anywhere in the galaxy.